6

Bernie Magruder and the Case of the Big Stink

Also by Phyllis Reynolds Naylor in Large Print:

Jade Green: A Ghost Story
Shiloh Season

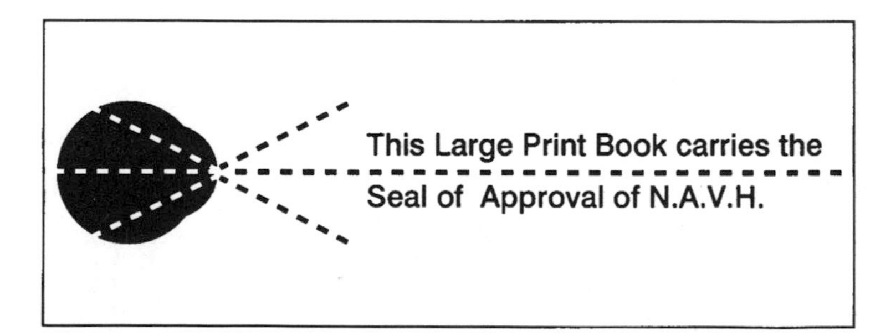

Bernie Magruder and the Case of the Big Stink

Phyllis Reynolds Naylor

Thorndike Press • Thorndike, Maine

Previously published as *The Mad Gasser of Bessledorf Street.*

Published in 2001 by arrangement with Simon & Schuster Children's Publishing Division

Thorndike Press Large Print Juvenile Series.

The text of this Large Print edition is unabridged.
Other aspects of the book may vary from the original edition.

Set in 16 pt. Plantin by Rick Gundberg.

Printed in the United States on permanent paper.

Library of Congress Cataloging-in-Publication Data

Naylor, Phyllis Reynolds.
[Mad gasser of Bessledorf Street]
Bernie Magruder & the case of the big stink / by Phyllis Reynolds Naylor.
p. cm.
Summary: Sam suspects the culprit who is gassing assembly line workers in the parachute factory lives in the hotel his family manages.
ISBN 0-7862-3134-3 (lg. print : hc : alk. paper)
1. Large type books. [1. Hotels, motels, etc. — Fiction. 2. Mystery and detective stories. 3. Large type books.]
I. Title: Bernie Magruder and the case of the big stink.
II. Title
PZ7.N24 Bi 2001
[Fic]—dc21 00-053622

For Ulysses and Marco

1

The Bessledorf Hotel was at 600 Bessledorf Street between the bus depot and the funeral parlor. Officer Feeney said that some folks came into town on one side of the hotel and exited on the other. The Bessledorf had thirty rooms, not counting the apartment where Bernie Magruder's family lived, and Feeney said the Mad Gasser could be in any one of them.

Bernie was in history class at school when it happened the first time. A police car went racing up Bessledorf Street, the siren wailing. Twenty-seven heads turned toward the window.

A second siren went by, and then a truck from the rescue squad, and twenty-seven bodies half rose from their seats, necks craned.

Three ambulances went by, and the whole class rushed to the window.

"I wonder," said Mr. Goldstein, "if we might pay a little attention to history?"

"History is being made right now down on Bessledorf Street, and we're missing out on it," said Bernie, not trying to be smart or anything.

"Then you'll read about it in the morning paper," said Mr. Goldstein, and motioned his students back to their seats.

Bernie was always bothered when sirens went south on Bessledorf because he worried about the hotel. His father had only been manager there for six months, and Bernie wanted things to work out. Before that, Mr. Magruder had been a house painter, an auctioneer, and a vacuum cleaner salesman; and the four Magruder children — Delores, Joseph, Bernie, and Lester — had been drifting around the country like dry leaves on a windy day, as Mother always said. Now they were here in Middleburg and Bernie wanted to stay.

The bell rang at last. Bernie hurried outside and started home. By the time Georgene Riley and Weasel caught up with him, the ambulances were coming back again, lights flashing. They turned down the road to the hospital.

Bernie stopped and watched until they were out of sight. Whatever it was, he had missed it.

"It couldn't have been an explosion," Weasel said, pushing up the glasses that kept sliding down his nose, "because we would have heard it."

"It couldn't have been a fire," said Georgene, her ponytail swinging, "or we'd smell the smoke."

"Well, if I find out, I'll call you," Bernie promised. They separated at the corner and Bernie went down the block alone. At least there weren't any police cars or fire trucks in front of the hotel.

He walked under the small canopy and through the double doors. Theodore Magruder, his father, was registering a guest at the front desk. Bernie went over to the television set in the lobby.

Old Mr. Lamkin was watching his favorite program, "No Tomorrow." He sat there in his purple cardigan sweater with one hand on each knee as a man on the screen told a woman he was leaving her for good. The woman started to cry, and Mr. Lamkin's chin trembled.

"Mr. Lamkin," Bernie whispered. "Could we try another channel for news?"

Mr. Lamkin's chin went on trembling.

Bernie sat down beside him, waiting politely. There was a break for a commercial about a new product called *Gone*:

"So strong, so thorough, so reliable that even the most stubborn stains come clean," the announcer said. "Use it on walls, on floors, or in the garage where grease and oil. . . ."

"Mr. Lamkin," said Bernie, "would you mind if I switched to Channel Three for a minute?"

"What's on Channel Three?" said Mr. Lamkin.

"Something awful's happened, and I want to find out what."

"Something awful's happening right here on 'No Tomorrow,' " said Mr. Lamkin. "That no-good Chet Hunsley is leaving Lora Lee to go raise chickens in Texas."

The program was on again. Bernie went around the front desk and through the door that led to the apartment behind. Lester, his nine-year-old brother, had reached home first and already had two fingers in the peanut butter jar. Lester was something of a slob, and Bernie suspected that if he ever tied a string around Lester and set him by the curb, the garbage truck would pick him up.

"What were those sirens about?" Bernie asked.

Lester shrugged, wiping his fingers on his shirt.

Bernie sat down and peeled a tangerine. He never got any help from Lester. But Joseph would be home soon from his classes at the veterinary college, and maybe he would know.

At that moment, however, there was a terrible shriek from the lobby, and Bernie ran toward it.

Twenty-year-old Delores, Bernie's sister, was staggering through the double doors, her face white, her eyes huge, and her mouth sagging.

"What's the matter?" asked her father. "Delores, my girl, what has happened?"

Just then Joseph came in the door behind her carrying two gray cats, who sprang from his arms and went crazy. One leaped to the top of the registration desk, and the other attached himself to Mr. Lamkin's purple cardigan.

"I've been gassed!" Delores gulped, and fell backward into the arms of her brother.

2

The hotel lobby was in a royal uproar. The two cats were everywhere, climbing up the draperies, scooting under couches, and prowling among the suitcases by the elevator.

Mrs. Magruder came to the door of the hotel dining room, where she was hostess, and when she saw her daughter slumped in the arms of Joseph, she rushed over to fan Delores's face.

"Grab those cats!" Theodore commanded, as the guest at the registration desk stared, open-mouthed.

Bernie grabbed the light-colored cat and Lester the dark one, and they shoved them in the broom closet, closing the door.

Joseph, meanwhile, was dragging his sister over to a couch in the lobby. Everyone rubbed her hands and tickled her feet until at last Delores opened her eyes. When she heard the announcer on television say "No Tomorrow," however, she blacked out again, and it wasn't until Mrs. Verona, the cook, held a bottle of vinegar under her nose that Delores sat up.

"I've been gassed," she said again.

"Nonsense, it's only vinegar," said Mrs. Verona.

"No," said Delores. "At the factory."

Bernie stared at his sister. Delores worked at the parachute factory at the far end of Bessledorf Street, attaching grommets to risers to harnesses, and she never did anybody any harm.

"Gassed?" repeated her father. "When?"

"An hour ago. First the girls in the mail room smelled it, then the women at the chute table, and finally it was all the way over to rip cords. Ida Mae Pinkhouse passed out, and then Claudia Stillmore started to choke, and by the time the ambulances got there, everyone was coughing and gagging and it was terrible! Five women were unconscious on the floor. Mr. Hokum opened all the windows and sent us home, and the police have started an investigation."

Bernie's eyes opened wide. "What did the gas smell like?" he wanted to know.

"Like rotten potatoes, ammonia, and sick cats," said Delores. "The worst thing I ever smelled in my life."

"Speaking of cats . . ." said Theodore, as the scratching and meowing in the broom closet grew more frantic. "Joseph, what were you thinking of? Two cats are all we need!"

Everyone turned to Joseph.

"I didn't know what else to do with them except bring them home," he said. "Somebody left them on the steps of the veterinary college in a pillowcase, and I found them just as I was leaving."

"Was there a note?" asked Bernie.

"No. Last month somebody left a rabbit, and the month before that it was a goldfish with a fin missing, and the month before that a Pekinese, so this time it was my turn to bring the little waifs home."

"Waifs, indeed!" said Mother, as the scratching continued.

"We'll just have to keep them," Joseph said. "My professor says that the world would be a better place if we got rid of the people and kept the animals, and he'll ask every day how they're doing."

"Well, if they're going to stay here, they've got to have names," Mrs. Magruder said, and the four Magruder offspring cheered.

"How about naming them after presidents?" said Theodore, whose thoughts were rather grand. "What about Hoover and Harding?"

"I should say not!" said his wife.

Delores, who was still looking a little pale around the eyes, said, "I think we should name them after poets."

"Byron and Keats," agreed Mother. But that didn't sound right to Bernie. Cats were neither poets nor presidents.

"I think we should name them after explorers because that's what they really are," he suggested.

"A wonderful idea!" said Theodore.

"Columbus!" said Lester.

"Balboa," said Mother.

"Cortez," said Delores, dreamily.

"No," said Joseph. "I found them and I'll name them. I'll call them Lewis and Clark."

So Lewis the Light and Clark the Dark were let out of the broom closet and taken back to the apartment. Bernie poured their milk and Lester fed them peanut butter, and they settled in.

That night, on the ten o'clock news, there was a story about the gassing in the parachute factory. The announcer said that five women had been rushed to the hospital that afternoon, but had recovered, and the investigation would continue.

3

Nothing happened the next day except that Lewis got into Mrs. Magruder's jewelry box and carried off an earring and Clark ate the leaves of the begonia plant.

On Saturday, however, Bernie got up early as he always did — just to be sure the hotel was still there — and was sweeping the sidewalk in front when Officer Feeney came along.

"Any more news about the gas at the parachute factory?" Bernie asked him.

Officer Feeney swung his nightstick around and around. "Well, maybe there is and maybe there isn't," he said, which was the way he always answered. "There weren't any gas leaks in the boiler room; weren't any gas leaks around the machines."

"So what do you think?" Bernie asked, resting on his broom.

"Well, I don't know about the rest of the police force, but *I'm* thinking it could be a new kind of gas, a strange kind of gas, that can't be picked up on an instrument — the kind of gas somebody could carry around and squirt under doors."

"Merciful heavens!" said a voice above them, where Mrs. Buzzwell was leaning out the window, listening.

Bernie lowered his voice.

"Why do you suppose someone would gas a parachute factory?"

"Well, I don't know what the rest of the force thinks," Feeney said again, "but *I'm* thinking maybe someone just meant to slip in a little, you know — enough to make the girls dizzy, so that the rip cords wouldn't be sewn on right or the grommets wouldn't hold or the bottoms of the chutes would be laced together."

"Who would do a thing like that?" Bernie gasped.

Officer Feeney thought it over. "Don't know what the rest of the force thinks, but it *could* be someone with a grudge against airplanes."

The policeman turned toward the bus depot and gave it a long, hard look: "And if that somebody came into town on a bus, where do you suppose he would stay?" With that, he twirled his nightstick again and sauntered off down to the corner.

Bernie stood staring after him. Feeney was probably right: it would have to be someone from outside, because Middleburg loved the factory. And if somebody *did* come to town to start trouble, and if that someone got arrested in the Bessledorf Hotel, Mr. Fairchild, the owner, would fire the Magruders. Of course, if Bernie Magruder were to catch the gasser red-handed, Mr. Fairchild would just have to be pleased.

When Bernie put the broom away in the closet, Mrs. Buzzwell was waiting for him.

"There's a Mad Gasser loose on Bessledorf Street, I just knew it!" she said in a voice like gravel going down a tin chute.

"That's only Officer Feeney's guess," Bernie told her, trying to stop whatever she was about to start. But stopping Mrs. Buzzwell was like trying to stop a bucket of water in midair. When Delores came downstairs from changing the sheets, she said that the whole third floor was talking about it. When Hildegarde, the cleaning woman, finished vacuuming the rooms, she said the story was spreading all over second. And it was the chief topic of conversation among the regulars in the hotel dining room at noon.

The Magruders discussed it over dinner back in the apartment. Bernie and Joseph, who looked like their father — brown hair, brown eyes, with rather large ears and high foreheads — sat on one side of the table. Delores and Lester who looked like their mother, with pointy chins and pink cheeks, sat on the other.

"The regulars are stirring up the other guests," said Mrs. Magruder to her brood. "Mr. Lamkin got out his Old World War I gas mask just in case; Felicity Jones is tying knots in a fifty-foot rope should anyone need to escape from a window; and Mrs. Buzzwell wants someone on guard duty all night long. We've got to put a stop to this nonsense or the Bessledorf Hotel will go out of business."

"Cats," said Joseph, chewing thoughtfully on his broccoli stick, "are extremely sensitive to smells. If there were ever gas in the hotel, they would set up an awful yowling."

"Good!" said Theodore. "I shall go right out and tell the tenants." He got up from the table and strode magnificently into the lobby where a handful of people were playing pinochle in one corner and Mr. Lamkin was talking to no one in particular about what he had done in the war.

"I just thought it would reassure you to know," Theodore said grandly, "that the Bessledorf Hotel has acquired two specialists in the art of gas detection. The team of Lewis and Clark is on duty twenty-four hours a day, and in the unlikely event that gas should seep into this hotel, they would alert us at once. So please, ladies and gentlemen, enjoy your evening without worrying about it."

"Why, he's talking about those blinking cats, he is!" Mr. Lamkin murmured to himself, but no one heard. And when Delores's boyfriend, Albert Oates, came to take her to the movies, it was just another peaceful evening at the Bessledorf.

Until sometime after midnight, that is . . .

4

Bernie was still awake. He had read the last two chapters of *Life on the Mississippi*, worked his math problems, and eaten a bag of pretzels. Then he did some pushups and finally crawled in the lower bunk beneath Lester. Once in a while he heard a gentle thud in the lobby where the cats were playing, and he smiled contentedly.

Mr. Magruder had decided that once the lights were out and the guests in bed, there was no reason why Lewis and Clark should not patrol the hotel — several good reasons, in fact, why they should.

Two pair of eyes watched as Delores and Albert came in from the movies, tiptoed over to a couch in the lobby and sat down. Delores took off her coat and Albert took off his. Albert put his arm around Delores, and she put her head on his shoulder. Delores "oohed" and Albert "aahed." Albert took off his tie and Delores kicked off her shoes, and everything might have gone well except for one thing: Albert Oates lit a cigar.

The cats did not know Albert Oates, and

they did not know his cigars. Furthermore, they did not care for the smell of his cheap Havana, and suddenly Lewis leaped onto Albert's shoulder to check the odor out. Albert, thinking he was about to be mugged, flung out one arm, sending Lewis flying through the air to land on Clark. Clark yowled, Delores shrieked, and Albert — thinking the assailant had attacked her next — lunged roaring across the couch to save her.

Bernie tumbled out of bed and was the first person to reach the lobby, but he was too late to stop what happened next.

Old Mr. Lamkin had heard the noise and smelled something strange. He rushed to the door of his room and called out into the hall, "Up! Up, everyone! The Mad Gasser is upon us!" and emerged seconds later in his robe, his slippers, and his World War I gas mask.

"Oh, no!" said Bernie.

Mrs. Buzzwell was the next person to reach the lobby, and when she saw Albert with his tie off and Delores with her shoes off, she huffed, "In *my* day we didn't take off anything at all until we were married!"

By the time Mr. and Mrs. Magruder and Joseph got out to the lobby, all the guests on first had been awakened, half the guests on second, and a few of the ones on third. Albert, of course, had put out his cigar at once, but the cats were still carrying on.

"What on earth are these cats doing in here?" demanded Mrs. Buzzwell.

Felicity Jones began to weep. "First there's a Mad Gasser loose on the street, and now it's animals loose in the hotel!"

"My good people," said Theodore, "may I introduce the trained animal team of Lewis and Clark. Not only are these fine feline specimens capable of sniffing out the most noxious of gasses, but they have proven themselves smoke detectors as well."

"In that case," said Felicity, "I think I shall go back to bed."

"I'll *try* to sleep," said Mrs. Buzzwell, "but any more commotion, and I'll find a new hotel."

"You can take off your gas mask, Mr. Lamkin," Bernie said to the old man and helped him back to his room.

"Delores, my dear," said her mother. "Do try not to make a fuss when you come in. Remember our guests."

"I'm dreadfully sorry, Mrs. Magruder, it won't happen again," said Albert Oates. "I shall never let a cigar touch my lips again."

"Good thinking!" said Theodore.

The Magruders all went back in the apartment and sat down at the table for ginger ale and Oreo cookies — all but Lester, who had slept through the whole thing.

"There's just one problem," said Joseph. "I'm not entirely sure that if it were an odorless gas, the cats would know it. What we really need is a canary."

"Like the ones that used to go down in the coal mines?" asked his father.

"Right. If the bird rolled over with its feet in the air, the miners knew that gas was present."

"Poor canaries," sniffled Delores.

On Monday, Joseph brought home a big green and yellow parrot named Salt Water, with one eye slightly closed and a few nicks in his beak. It wasn't a canary, but it was the only bird that had been left on the steps of the veterinary college, and it would have to do.

Bernie was delighted. Life in Middleburg was really working out. First two cats and now a parrot! But Mrs. Magruder frowned disapprovingly.

"Isn't he rather mangy-looking, Joseph?"

"Zip your lip, zip your lip," said Salt Water.

The Magruders stared.

"Well," sighed Mrs. Magruder finally, "I guess we'll have to keep him. There is one consolation, however. If the Mad Gasser ever *does* decide to gas our hotel, Salt Walter will be the first to go."

5

Pets, however, did not keep Bernie from worrying. There was either a Mad Gasser loose in the neighborhood or a wild rumor of a Mad Gasser, and Bernie wasn't sure which was worse. Rumors could put the Bessledorf out of business as surely as a madman himself.

"It seems to me," said Georgene Riley at lunch time on Monday, "that if there *is* a Mad Gasser and he came to town on the bus and he took a room at the Bessledorf, you'd know."

"*How* would I know?" asked Bernie.

"The eyes," said Georgene. "You'd be able to tell by looking."

"Well, I'm going to check out the registration book," said Bernie. "It would probably be someone who signed in just before the gassing happened."

When Bernie got home from school, he found Salt Water on a new perch in the lobby. It was just high enough off the floor that the cats couldn't reach him.

"Go back, Jack. Go back, Jack," squawked the parrot.

"He's been talking a blue streak all day and all of it nonsense," said Bernie's father.

Bernie went over to the desk. "Want me to take over for a while, Dad? Give you a break?"

"That's a good idea," said Theodore. "I'd like to go to the hardware store and get some new locks for the windows."

Bernie sat down on the stool behind the desk. He sorted all the mail and stuck it in the proper slots. He took a phone message, got a complaint about a leaky faucet, called Wilbur Wilkins, the handyman, and had room service take a cup of cocoa to Felicity Jones.

When all was quiet at last, Bernie turned the pages of the guest book back to Sept. 29 to see who had registered just before the gassing of the parachute factory. There were only three names:

Thomas Valrugo, room 301
Hazel Sutton, room 205
Jack Martin, room 212

"Go back, Jack. Go back, Jack," squawked Salt Water.

When Theodore Magruder came home from the hardware store and took over the desk again, the phone rang and he answered.

"Certainly. . . . Of course, Mr. Martin," Theodore said. "I'll send someone up right away." He hung up. "Bernie, the man in 212 wants someone to go to the drugstore for him. Can you do it?"

"Sure!" Bernie said eagerly, and took the elevator to second.

Jack Martin was a huge man, with dark bushy brows. His eyes, what Bernie could see of them, were ringed with red. He wore a turtleneck shirt and a sweater over that and an overcoat over the sweater. The pockets in his overcoat bulged ominously. He looked very, very strange.

"Here's a list and here's a fiver," Jack Martin said. "See how fast you can get back here, boy."

Bernie set off at a run.

He read the list on the stairs going down: alcohol, camphor, petroleum jelly, and glycerin drops. *Very strange indeed.* On the way to the drugstore, he ran into Weasel.

"Come on," Bernie said. "I've got a suspect. Just look at this list."

"Maybe he's making a bomb," Weasel said, reading it. "What's he look like?"

"Red eyes, bulging pockets, big coat," Bernie told him.

They bought the things on the list and ran all the way back to the hotel. Bernie knocked on the door of 212.

Jack Martin opened the door and peered

out. Then he reached into his pocket and pulled out a handkerchief, covering his face.

"Thank you," he said quickly to Bernie, taking the package. "Keep the change."

Bernie looked down at the two cents in his hand. "Thanks," he murmured.

The boys went down the hall to the elevator.

"What do you think?" asked Bernie.

"Something sick about him, all right," said Weasel. "Like a cold."

When they walked out into the lobby, Mr. Magruder was on the phone again:

"Yes, Mr. Martin. Certainly. I'd recommend Dr. Goddard. I'll call and see if he can't get over this afternoon." When he hung up, Mr. Magruder looked over at Bernie: "The man in 212 has a bad cold and wants a doctor to see him."

Weasel looked at Bernie disgustedly. "Wow! Thanks for letting me in on all the excitement!" he said, and went home.

Well, not everybody's lucky the first time, Bernie told himself. *I've still got Thomas Valrugo and Hazel Sutton to check out.*

That evening, Theodore Magruder went off to sing with his Monday-night barbershop quartet, while Joseph took over the front desk.

One by one the guests left the dining hall, until there was only Mr. Lamkin left, finishing his rice pudding. The waiters put the chairs up on the tables and began vacuuming the floor. Out in the lobby, guests yawned and moved toward the elevator to go upstairs.

No one saw the unmarked truck that was coming down the back alley; no one saw it stop there by the trash cans of the Bessledorf Hotel. Not even Bernie.

6

Felicity Jones said goodnight to Mrs. Buzzwell at the elevator and went down the hall to her room. She read two poems from a book called *Dew Drops*, rubbed her face with cold cream, and turned out the light.

The moon was so brilliant, however, that she had to stand at the window a moment, sighing.

"Oh, lovely moon! Oh, beauteous moon! How gently dost thou glide . . ." she whispered.

At that moment she saw a man in a hooded jacket get out of an unmarked truck near the trash cans and cautiously make his way toward the back door of the hotel. He carried something big and bulky under one arm and something long and thin under the other. As Felicity watched, he went up to the hotel's dining room window and peered inside. Then finally, stealthily, he tiptoed to the back door and slowly pushed it open.

Meanwhile, in the Magruder apartment, Bernie's mother was working on her novel. Mrs. Magruder wrote books in her spare time, but never got them published. She claimed to have the largest collection of rejection slips in the United States and was using them to paper the hall closet. She was already up to the coat hangers and had the ceiling yet to go. On this particular Monday night she sat at her typewriter, the manuscript spread out around her. Bernie, sitting at the table beside her, was trying to think of a plan to flush out the Mad Gasser, and Lester was making himself a potato-chip sandwich.

"I wonder," said Mrs. Magruder, "what a heroine would do if she was standing at the edge of a cliff and the killer was coming up the only road to the top."

"Jump off," said Lester, licking his fingers.

"Maybe she could climb over the edge and lower herself down with a rope," Bernie suggested, imagining *himself* at the top of a cliff and the Mad Gasser after him.

"Well, I know what *I* would do if I were standing on the edge of a cliff with a killer on the loose," said Delores. "I'd scream."

At that precise moment, a scream fractured the Monday night quiet. It sounded like someone scratching on a blackboard in stereo.

"What on earth . . . ?" gasped Mrs. Magruder, jumping up, and they all ran into the lobby.

Felicity Jones burst out the door of her room in her bathrobe and rushed down the hall, her face smeared with cold cream.

"It's him!" she shrieked. "The Mad Gasser!"

"Where?" asked Joseph from behind the front desk.

"Coming in the back door near the hotel kitchen."

"Oh, my stars, and your father's not here!" Mrs. Magruder said to her children.

Mr. Lamkin appeared in the hallway in his gas mask. This time he was also waving a sword.

"Where is he?" came his muffled voice from beneath the mask.

"Put that thing away," said Mother. "Felicity, what did the man look like? It *was* a man, I presume?"

"He's wearing a hooded jacket," said Felicity tearfully, "and he has something big and bulky under one arm and something long and thin under the other."

"Bernie, call the police and tell them to come at once," Mrs. Magruder said. And then, turning to Joseph, she said anxiously, "The cook is still there! Someone's got to protect her."

"Don't worry," said Joseph, picking up a fly swatter. "I'll get him!" He walked boldly into the dining room and toward the kitchen doors beyond.

Bernie called the police and then stood guard with Lester, should the Mad Gasser come charging into the lobby. Felicity Jones locked herself in her room, and Mr. Lamkin paced back and forth in his gas mask.

Mrs. Magruder began to sniffle. "I never thought, when we took this hotel, that it would come to this," she said weeping.

There was the sound of a scuffle, a shout, a roar, and then an enormous clatter of pots and pans. Bernie raced toward the hotel kitchen to help his brother just as Officer Feeney came in the front door.

"Hello, Jack! Hello, Jack!" squawked Salt Water.

A heap of pots and pans lay on the kitchen floor with a pair of feet sticking out. Bernie grabbed a foot and held on so the man couldn't escape. Joseph, panting, leaned against the refrigerator, and Mrs. Verona, the cook, stood with arms folded, looking very pleased with herself.

"Now what's all this?" said Officer Feeney.

"The Mad Gasser, that's what," said Mrs. Verona. "Joseph zapped him, and I trapped him with my pots and pans. I just opened the cupboard above the stove, and they all fell out."

The heap of pots and pans began to move. One arm came out, then another, and finally a man sat up, with Bernie still holding onto his shoe.

"Oh, merciful heavens," said Mother. "It's Clyde, the exterminator!"

"A blinking circus, that's what this is!" said Clyde, rubbing his head. Bernie let go, and the man got to his feet, picking up his pesticide and nozzle. "Come after dark, you said, after the dining room was empty so I wouldn't upset your guests. Well, I sat out in the truck a half hour waitin' for the bloody lights to go out in the dining room while some old man finishes his rice pudding, and just as I gets my chance to slip inside, Joseph here whacks me with the swatter."

"Oh, dear," said Mrs. Magruder. She turned to Officer Feeney. "The guests get terribly upset when they see an exterminator."

"Next time," said Clyde, "I'm walkin' in the front door, right through the lobby, and I'll say, 'Excuse me, Ma'am,' and spray right under the tables. No more sneakin' in the back door."

He sprayed around the kitchen and dining room, and then he went banging out the door in a huff. Officer Feeney shook his head.

"Good thing he didn't press charges," he

said to Joseph. "Could have got you for assault and battery."

"If you policemen would capture that madman, things like this wouldn't happen," Mrs. Magruder said with a pout.

"We're working on it, ma'am," said Officer Feeney, and he went back outside.

The Magruders returned to their apartment.

"Albert will never ask me to marry him if things like this keep happening." Delores sniffled.

"Nonsense," said her mother. "There's nothing that makes a young man more protective of a woman than to feel that he is rescuing her from her own family."

Mrs. Magruder went back to her manuscript, and Delores finished polishing her nails. But Bernie sat at the window trying to sort things through. All he could come up with was that there might be a mad gasser loose, and if there was, he might be in the Bessledorf. That was enough for Bernie. He had to keep looking.

7

Bernie's social studies class was starting a unit on communication. Everyone had to write a report on the telegraph, the telephone, or the radio. Bernie bent over his desk, with the *World Book Encyclopedia*, writing a report on Samuel Morse and the telegraph. He was looking at the arrangement of dots and dashes of the International Morse code that made up the letters of the alphabet. When he got up to sharpen his pencil, he passed Weasel's desk and noticed that Weasel had the other "M" encyclopedia and was looking at the Morse code, too.

Bernie went back to his desk and caught Weasel's eye. Then he softly tapped out a message with his pencil: a tap was a dot; a scrape of his pencil along the edge of his desk was a dash. After each letter, he left a long pause so that Weasel could look it up and write it down, and an even longer pause at the end of a word: W (one dot, two dashes), E (one dot), A (one dot, one dash) . . . *Weasel is a jerk.*

Weasel grinned as he deciphered the last

word, then tapped out a message of his own: S (three dots), O (three dashes) . . . *So is Bernie.*

"If the two boys who are sending compliments to each other don't cut it out, they will spend tomorrow's lunch hour in detention," Mr. Goldstein said, without even looking up.

Bernie bent over his paper again, and it was then he heard a siren. He could just see the top of the squad car as it sped by beneath the windows. It did not turn on Fairmont or Maine or Corning, but went straight up Bessledorf.

Bernie could almost tell just by listening how far the cruiser had gone. Now it would be passing the funeral parlor, now the hotel and the bus depot. . . .

The wailing went on. It was going up the hill toward the parachute factory.

Another siren, the rescue squad, and again, the three ambulances. The whole class rose from their seats and dashed to the windows, and Mr. Goldstein didn't even try to stop them.

Bernie felt sick. He looked at the clock. Same time as last week. Thursday. Same *day.* The Mad Gasser had struck again.

The intercom clicked on, and the principal's voice came over the speaker:

"Teachers and students, I would like your attention. We have just learned from the police department that there has been another gassing at the parachute factory. Since we do not know what it is or what may happen next, we have been advised to dismiss our classes early. . . ."

A large cheer went up from the students.

". . . and instruct each of you to go directly home. I repeat: go directly home."

Bernie started running the minute he left school.

"I don't care what the principal says," he told Weasel and Georgene. "I'm going to the factory. My sister may still be in there."

"We'll come with you," Georgene said.

They headed toward the crowd that was gathering up on the hill. Even before they got to the top, ambulances, their lights flashing, were starting to drive the workers to the hospital. When Bernie and Georgene and Weasel reached the rope that the police had stretched across the sidewalk, Bernie could see women lying out on the grass, some with oxygen masks over their faces.

"I'll bet it's sewer gas, backing up the pipes," someone in the crowd said to another.

A man shook his head. "They don't find out soon, the workers are going to quit, the factory's going to close, and it'll be a sad day for Middleburg when the parachute factory's gone."

Bernie's father was in the crowd when Delores came out between two officers, a handkerchief over her nose. He leaped over the rope and rushed to her.

"This is my daughter," he said to the policemen, and shook Delores gently. "Say something, my girl. Are you all right?"

Delores coughed some more.

"We'll need a statement from the young lady if she's up to it," one of the officers said. "What was the smell like, miss? Can you describe it?"

"Oh, it was awful!" Delores said, rolling her eyes. "Like rotten potatoes and ammonia and sick cats and sour cream."

The policeman wrote it all down.

"It's a disgrace, is what it is!" said Theodore. "These young girls are on the verge of having their lives snuffed out, and the Mad Gasser keeps coming back. How can he get in the place without anyone seeing him?"

"Well, it's a sticky business, it is," said the officer. "Could be he fires it through the window from a passing car. Could be it's a gas bomb detonated by remote control. Could be. . . ."

Just then Delores's boyfriend charged through the crowd, and Delores fell into his arms, sobbing.

"Let me take you away from all this," said

Albert Oates, kissing her on the forehead.

"Oh, Albert!" said Delores. "Is that a proposal?"

"Yes, my dear Delores. Let me take you away."

"In what?" Delores said, drying her eyes.

"My 1967 Buick."

Delores sniffed uncertainly. "To where?"

"Hoboken, New Jersey, my dear, to live happily ever after."

"Doing what?" said Delores.

"We can work side by side in my uncle's suspenders factory," said Albert, nuzzling her ear.

"To Hoboken, New Jersey, in a 1967 Buick, to work in a suspenders factory?" said Delores, and she began to cry again.

Bernie walked away. He could not understand how Delores and Albert could possibly be talking about suspenders when it was obvious that something awful was happening in Middleburg.

"I've got an idea," he said as he and Georgene and Weasel started back down the hill. "What smells as bad as rotten potatoes, ammonia, sick cats, and sour cream?"

"Your brother Lester," said Weasel.

"Besides him," said Bernie.

"I don't know," said Georgene. "What?"

"Embalming fluid," Bernie whispered.

“You think the Mad Gasser is using embalming fluid?” Georgene asked.

“He might even be one of the morticians,” said Bernie. “Come on.”

8

"What are we going to do at the funeral parlor?" Weasel wanted to know.

"Try to get in," said Bernie.

"What do we do if we can?" Georgene insisted.

Bernie was thinking. "Well, first we'll have to get down to the room where they prepare the bodies and see if the embalming fluid really does smell that awful."

When they reached the funeral home, however, there was a funeral in progress. Coming out the side door were six tall men in black suits carrying a casket. With somber faces, they slid it into the open door of the waiting hearse.

After the pall bearers came the flower carriers, and they picked up the baskets and wreaths and floral sprays and put them in a second car.

After the flower carriers came the mourners, dressed in gray and navy blue, dabbing at their eyes. The tall men with the somber faces and black suits opened the doors of the other cars and helped the people inside. Then they got in the cars themselves and slowly the procession moved down the street toward the cemetery.

When the last car had disappeared, Bernie and Weasel and Georgene went around to the back door of the funeral home and gently opened it. There were stairs going up and stairs going down.

Bernie had just moved toward the basement when a big black suit blocked the way and a big deep voice said, "Yes?"

Bernie gulped. There had been so many dark suits in the funeral procession he didn't imagine there could be any left.

"Uh . . . Bessledorf Hotel?" he asked.

"Next door," said the huge man with the somber face, and ushered them back outside.

"Any more bright ideas?" said Weasel.

Bernie kicked hard at a tin can in the alley.

"I'd better get home," Georgene said. "Mom will be worried." She and Weasel both left.

Bernie walked glumly around to the front door of the hotel. The minute he stepped inside, he knew that something was up, because Hildegarde was washing the windows as fast as she could go and Lester was polishing the doorknobs.

"What's happening?" Bernie asked.

"Mr. Fairchild just called from the airport. He's on his way over here, and Mom's been looking for you." Lester pulled a Hershey, which had been sat on, from his back pocket, stuffed half of it in his mouth, and went on polishing.

"Bernie!" Mrs. Magruder said when she saw him. "Take the vacuum and do the carpet quickly. Mr. Fairchild will be here any moment! Oh, I do wish Joseph would hurry and get home."

Delores came out of the apartment with an ice bag on her head to dust the potted plant, and Theodore was rushing about giving instructions to the waiters in the dining room.

Fifteen minutes later, the double doors opened, and Robert L. Fairchild, owner of the Bessledorf Hotel, swept inside. He wore a gray flannel suit and a red and blue tie and a watch chain that swung from his vest pocket with every step.

"Harumph," he said, and looked around.

"Welcome to the Bessledorf, Mr. Fairchild," said Theodore. "Would you like a cup of coffee here in the lobby, or perhaps you would care to dine early?"

"At the moment," said Mr. Fairchild, "I would like nothing more than the assurance that my hotel is in good hands and the madman I have been reading about in the papers cannot get in."

"My good sir," said Theodore proudly, "I

have taken every conceivable precaution. I have bought new locks for the windows, and the front door is bolted each night at midnight. Only guests have the key. Should the Mad Gasser still find his way inside, however, we have two cats, expert in both gas and smoke detection, and a parrot who would doubtless fall off his perch with the slightest hint of odorless gas."

Mr. Fairchild fixed his eyes on the parrot. "Not enough," he said. "We need something to keep a madman or a burglar or an arsonist or whatever from getting into the hotel at all." He began pacing back and forth across the lobby. "An electronic alarm system is too expensive, and I certainly cannot afford to hire a guard."

Just at that moment the front door opened and a huge dog, almost as tall as Mr. Fairchild himself, ambled in. It had short hair, the color of sand, and its long legs seemed disjointed at the tops, bending every which way at the hip sockets.

The Magruders stared. Mr. Fairchild stared. Then Joseph came in, looking sheepish.

9

Perhaps it was the sight of the parrot or possibly the presence of Lewis and Clark, but the Great Dane stretched his neck and began to howl. It was the loudest howl Bernie had ever heard.

"Don't tell me," said Theodore to Joseph. "Someone left him on the steps of the veterinary college."

Joseph nodded. "We heard him around lunchtime, and found him tied to the railing. No collar, no tag, so he can't be traced."

Mr. Fairchild walked around and around the big animal. "Hmmm," he kept saying.

"He must eat five pounds of food a day!" gasped Mrs. Magruder.

"Still," said Mr. Fairchild, "the cook surely has five pounds of scraps left over from dinner, and that's a lot cheaper than an electronic alarm system or a twenty-four-hour guard. Does he bark?"

Joseph looked at the dog. "Bark," he said.

The Great Dane continued to howl.

At that moment Lewis and Clark decided

they had had enough, and leaped out of Delores's arms.

The Dane was after them in a flash, barking and braying and racing madly down the hall.

"Shake a leg! Shake a leg!" squawked Salt Water.

The elevator door opened, and Mrs. Buzzwell stepped out. The dog went racing by, and Mrs. Buzzwell backed up against the wall.

"Oh, my stars!" she gasped. "What next?"

"My good woman," said Mr. Fairchild, "you are looking at a living alarm system that might one day save your life."

"Well!" said Mrs. Buzzwell.

"Furthermore," said Mr. Fairchild to Theodore, "you are to be commended for the excellent care you are taking of my hotel. I shall raise your salary ten dollars a week with a bonus at Christmas. However . . ." And he lowered his voice. "If the Mad Gasser, whoever he is, creates a problem in this hotel, you and your family will be out on the sidewalk, animals and all."

And with that, Mr. Fairchild tipped his hat, turned, and strode back out the door to the waiting taxi.

Bernie tried to imagine his family sitting out on the sidewalk with all their clothes and dishes, two cats, one parrot, and a Great

Dane. He knew that they would have to find the Mad Gasser before he found them.

Mrs. Magruder was still staring at the dog.

"Well," she said. "I guess he's a mixed blessing."

"That's it!" cried the four younger Magruders. "Mixed Blessing! That's his name."

"But where on earth will he sleep?" she said.

"How about the mat just inside the double doors?" suggested Joseph. "That's where we would want him if anyone tried to sneak in."

So the king-size mat inside the front door became the dog's bed. Guests had to step over him coming in and going out, but they didn't complain because he was guarding their lives.

During the evening meal, Mixed Blessing sat patiently outside the door of the dining room until all the guests had gone and old Mr. Lamkin had finished his custard. Then he bounced out to the kitchen, and ate the remains of the beef burgundy, some onion soup, a plate of peas, and a pumpkin pie.

The following day after school, Bernie was hanging around the bus depot when the bus from Chicago pulled in. He watched as people got off. The last to leave was a stocky man in a blue overcoat, carrying two suitcases and a satchel beneath his arm.

"Excuse me," the man said, walking up to Bernie. "Could you direct me to the Bessledorf Hotel?"

"Sure," Bernie told him. "It's right next door. My dad's the manager. Come on."

"Splendid," said the man. They went to the hotel, stepping over Mixed Blessing, there on the mat, and up to the registration desk.

"A room with a view," the man said to Bernie's father.

"Certainly," said Theodore. "Here is the key to 315, with a view of Bessledorf Hill."

"What is on Bessledorf Hill?" asked the stranger.

"Well, there's City Hall, the Majestic Theater, the bowling alley, and — at the top — the Bessledorf Parachute Factory."

"Very good," said the stranger again, and signed his name in the guest book. Bernie peeped at it over his shoulder. *John Doe.*

Bernie carried the suitcase, and he and the man went up the elevator to third. The man unlocked the door to 315 and went over to the window. "Ah," he said.

"I hope you'll be comfortable," said Bernie. "Just call the desk if you need anything."

"Thank you," said John Doe, and gave him a dime.

When Bernie went back downstairs, his father was still looking at the name in the guest book, shaking his head.

"John Doe," he said. "Why, I could think up a better name myself. He's a detective if I ever saw one. Probably sent by the FBI to help find the Mad Gasser."

Bernie went over and leaned on Salt Water's perch. His heart thumped excitedly. If the FBI sent a detective here, that could only mean that a suspect was close at hand.

Bernie checked the guest list again. It couldn't be Jack Martin, because his cold had become the flu, and he'd been in bed all week. That left Hazel Sutton and Thomas Valrugo. It was comforting, in a way, to have an FBI man in the hotel, but Bernie had secretly hoped to capture the Mad Gasser himself. Maybe, if he followed John Doe around for a few days, he'd learn something about being a detective.

10

"He doesn't look like a detective to me," said Georgene.

Bernie, Georgene, and Weasel were sitting on a couch in the lobby, when John Doe came down for lunch on Saturday.

"Why not?" asked Bernie.

"He needs a pipe — one that's shaped like a saxophone," said Georgene.

"And a checkered cap," said Weasel.

"That's just the point," said Bernie. "He doesn't look like a detective at all, so no one would ever guess. And what detective goes around calling himself John Doe?"

They watched while the man bought a morning paper from the stack near the front desk and took it into the dining room. Now and then they sauntered by the door to see what he was doing. He was stirring his coffee with his left hand and holding the newspaper with his right.

Bernie and his friends sat back down.

A few minutes later, John Doe came through the lobby again. He stepped over the dog and went outside, looked around, and started up Bessledorf Street toward the hill.

"See?" said Bernie. "He wants to look over the parachute factory, I'll bet — see if he can find any clues. Listen. We ought to take this chance and check out his room. See what kind of equipment he uses — spy glasses and stuff."

"You mean you can go in people's rooms?" Georgene asked.

"Only if I'm working. I can't touch anything that belongs to them or open any drawers, but I can look around."

"How would you get in?"

"I'll ask Hildegarde if she needs any help. She always says yes."

They started for the elevator.

"There's just one thing," said Bernie. "We need somebody for the lookout. Georgene, why don't you stay down here and let us know when he's coming back."

"Why do *I* have to be the lookout?" she demanded.

"Just this once. Next time someone else will do it."

Georgene scowled and plopped back down on the couch.

Bernie and Weasel went up to third floor to find Hildegarde. She was just coming down the hall with her cart — mops, buckets, and brooms sticking out the sides.

"Need some help?" Bernie called.

"Sure," said Hildegarde, "but you better do a good job. Why don't you take the feather dusters and do all the rooms? I'll come behind you with the vacuum sweeper." She gave Bernie the keys.

The boys started in room 313 so it wouldn't be too obvious. They finally reached room 315 and went inside.

A few shirts and trousers were hanging neatly in the closet. One pair of shoes lay on the floor beneath, and an umbrella and suitcases were sitting on the shelf above. The suitcases were closed. The satchel lay on the desk. It was closed, too.

Bernie and Weasel went over the room dusting everything twice, but there was nothing at all to see — not a map or a badge or a gun or a magnifying glass in sight.

They were starting to dust for the third time when Georgene stuck her head in the door. "He's coming!" she whispered.

Bernie and Weasel went out in the hall, and Bernie locked the door behind him. They had just dropped the feather dusters back in the cart when Hildegarde poked her head out of 314.

"Hey! You can't be through already!"

"We just thought of something else to do," Bernie said.

Hildegarde blocked the hallway. "Oh, no,

you don't! Nobody does half a job for Hildegarde. You said you'd dust, and you're not finished till you've done the third floor!"

Bernie and Weasel turned helplessly to Georgene, but she was waving goodbye.

"Have a good time," she said sweetly, and pressed the button for the elevator.

Bernie sighed, and went on dusting. A half hour later, the boys were done.

Weasel hunched his shoulders as they went downstairs and thrust his glasses back up on his nose. "Do me a favor," he said. "You get any more ideas, you keep them to yourself."

Bernie was disgusted too. When he went to bed later and found that cracker crumbs had drifted down from Lester's bunk, he roared, "Lester, you're leaking all over the place! You're a real pig!"

The room was quiet, and then a small voice came from the top bunk: "Am I breathing too loud for you, Bernie?"

Bernie was ashamed. He was just frustrated that nothing had happened and was taking it out on Lester.

But the next morning something did happen. When Bernie went out into the lobby early to open the drapes, he found that Salt Water had fallen off his perch and was lying on the floor, legs in the air, not moving a feather.

11

Bernie's first thought was that Lewis and Clark had done the bird in. But the meowing behind the basement door told him that the cats had been accidentally locked in the basement, and had stayed there all night.

He looked at Mixed Blessing, but the huge dog was backing away from Salt Water and whining. There were no marks of any kind on the parrot's body, and Bernie could see the heart still beating in the upturned breast.

The Mad Gasser. Who else?

He dashed back into the apartment where the family was just beginning to stir.

"Gas!" he yelled. "Odorless gas! Salt Water's fallen off his perch, but he's still breathing!"

"Oh, my word!" cried Mrs. Magruder.

Delores dropped the toast she was buttering. "I can feel it! I can feel it!" she said. "I'm getting all lightheaded."

"Open the windows!" Theodore commanded. "Bernie, get everybody out on first floor. Joseph, you take second, and I'll take third. Lester, get your sister out onto the sidewalk."

Bernie pounded on Mr. Lamkin's door.

"Mr. Lamkin! Get out! There's gas in the hotel!"

Mr. Lamkin burst through the door, half asleep, fumbling with his gas mask, and got it on backwards.

Someone let the cats out of the basement, and they were so distraught that Lewis leaped on the potted plant and Clark hid in the mail-bag under the front desk.

Mr. Magruder had not wanted to phone the police until he could be sure what was what, but when Felicity Jones was carried through the lobby in a swoon and Mrs. Buzzwell collapsed inside the front door, Bernie's mother called headquarters:

"We've been gassed," she said hoarsely. "The Bessledorf Hotel."

John Doe came running over to the desk as Bernie was gathering up Lewis and Clark to take them outside.

"Is everybody out?" he asked.

"Yes, thank goodness," said Mother. "Theodore has made a check of every room, and I hear the fire trucks coming now."

"A shame!" John Doe said. "A shame, that's what it is, when ordinary citizens can't stay in an ordinary hotel without being gassed."

Mrs. Magruder started to weep. She looked

at all the guests standing out on the sidewalk and imagined her family and furniture and dishes on the sidewalk, too. When Robert L. Fairchild heard about this, he would fire the whole Magruder clan and choose someone else as manager. "We've done the very best we can," she sobbed.

"My dear Mrs. Magruder, I didn't mean to imply that you hadn't. Do come outside."

Somehow, in all the confusion, the Magruders managed to get Mixed Blessing and the cats out, but Salt Water was still in the lobby. Joseph went back for the parrot and brought him out wrapped in a dinner napkin.

"Move back! Move back! Give him air!" said Theodore, as Joseph laid the bird on the hood of the car. The little heart was still beating.

Bernie watched as Joseph bent down and examined Salt Water carefully. He lifted his wings, rotated his drumsticks, pried open his beak, and lifted his eyelid with one thumb.

"Will he be all right?" Bernie asked his brother.

Joseph just frowned.

The rescue squad arrived and barged into the lobby with gas masks. The Fire Chief and Police Inspector went inside carrying gas detectors, and came back out a few minutes later.

"No sign of gas anywhere," they said.

"Oh, thank heaven!" said Mother.

"But how do we explain *that?*" said Officer Feeney, pointing to the heap of legs and arms there on the sidewalk belonging to Felicity Jones, Mrs. Buzzwell, and Delores.

"Looks like they tried a tackle and knocked each other out," said the Fire Chief.

"They were carried from this building unconscious!" Mother insisted hotly.

"Well," said the Police Inspector, "if it *is* gas, it's something new, and nothing we can detect on our monitors."

"And what am I supposed to tell the owner of this hotel?" asked Theodore.

"We'll call it a false alarm," said the Fire Chief, and wrote it down in his report. "Put the cats back, and if they're all right after fifteen minutes, then everyone can go inside."

So Lewis and Clark were allowed back in the lobby, and while the guests watched through the windows, they frolicked on the registration desk and checked out all the mail slots. When fifteen minutes were up, Felicity Jones and Mrs. Buzzwell and Delores were escorted back in, and Mr. Lamkin took off his gas mask.

Bernie and Joseph put Salt Water in an old wool golf cap beneath a forty-watt bulb, and by the next morning he was back on his perch, scolding the cats and squawking, "Rise and shine! Rise and shine!"

"I believe it was just a rare twenty-four hour virus peculiar to Panamanian parrots," Joseph said. "He wasn't gassed at all."

"I'm glad to hear it!" said Mother.

"But Felicity Jones and Mrs. Buzzwell . . . !" Bernie protested.

Joseph shook his head. "I just can't explain it."

That night, however, Delores Magruder opened her purse and found a piece of folded paper inside. The note read:

> TO WHOM IT MAY CONCERN:
> THE GASSING OF THE PARACHUTE FACTORY WAS ONLY THE BEGINNING. TELL THE MAYOR THAT I HAVE ENOUGH GAS FOR EVERY BUILDING IN MIDDLEBURG. FOR TEN-THOUSAND DOLLARS I WILL LEAVE TOWN AND TAKE MY FORMULA WITH ME.
>
> THE MAD GASSER
> OF BESSLEDORF STREET

12

Delores Magruder lay on the couch, her mother fanning her, while Officer Feeney and the Police Inspector asked questions. Every now and then her eyes rolled back, and Bernie stuck the vinegar under her nose again.

"To think," Delores whispered, "that the Mad Gasser actually had his hands in my purse."

The Police Inspector was a tall man with tufts of gray hair sticking out of his ears. A pair of rimless spectacles pinched his nose as he jotted down things in a notebook.

"When you arrived at work this morning, what did you do with your pocketbook?" he asked.

"Put it under the bench like the other girls do."

"Did you open it at all during the day?"

"Now and then, I suppose," Delores answered.

"And when you left the factory to come home, did you open it at that time?"

"No, because I didn't take the bus. I got a ride."

"With whom?" asked the Inspector.

Delores frowned at the question.

"My dear, please answer," begged Mrs. Magruder. "You could have accepted a ride from the Mad Gasser himself, for all we know."

"It was a gas, all right," said Delores, sitting up and folding her arms over her chest. "It was my boyfriend — my *ex*-boyfriend — Albert Oates."

"Oh, Delores!" cried Mrs. Magruder. "Does that mean the wedding is off?"

"Do you want your only daughter to move to Hoboken, New Jersey, Mother, to spend the rest of her natural life in a suspenders factory?" said Delores.

"Ladies, if you please . . ." said the Inspector, clearing his throat. He turned to Delores. "I know that this is a delicate question, and I am terribly sorry to embarrass you in any way, but did this Mr. Oates, at any time, put his hands on your purse?"

"He did not," said Delores. "I sat as far away from him as I could get without falling out the door."

"And he did not, at any time, so much as touch your pocketbook?"

"Well," said Delores, "my purse touched him. Just before I got out of the car, I whacked him with it."

The Police Inspector wrote it all down. "When you arrived here at the hotel, Miss Magruder, what did you do with your purse then?"

Delores tried to think. "Well, I put it down on the front desk when I hugged Lewis."

"Another boyfriend?" asked the Inspector.

"A cat," Bernie corrected.

"Then I went behind the desk to see if I had any mail," Delores said.

"And left your purse lying there?"

"I suppose so."

"Do you remember who was in the lobby?"

"I just didn't notice," said Delores.

The Inspector went out in the lobby to look around.

"What do you think?" Bernie asked Officer Feeney.

"Well, I don't know what the Inspector thinks, but *I* suspect it's an inside job," said Feeney.

"Someone inside this hotel?"

"Maybe yes and maybe no," said Feeney. "A lot can happen to a purse when you turn your back."

"You probably think that I wrote the note myself," said Delores, starting to weep again.

"Can't you check the handwriting?" suggested Bernie.

"Isn't handwriting," Feeney said, studying

the note. "Printed in big block letters with blue ink on white paper — cheap tablet paper, the kind you can buy anywhere."

After the police had gone, Bernie went out to the lobby and tried to remember who had been there since he got home from school. Old Mr. Lamkin had been watching television as usual because Bernie remembered the commercial for *Gone*: "So strong, so thorough, so reliable that even the most stubborn stains come clean. . . ." Thomas Valrugo had been working a crossword puzzle in the corner and John Doe had been making a phone call over by the elevator. At some point a woman came in or went out, Bernie wasn't sure. He realized how difficult it was to remember details when you didn't know at the time how important they might be.

"Why Delores?" Mrs. Magruder said at dinner. "Why, of all people in Middleburg, did the Mad Gasser choose us? Theodore, I could not bear it if you had to go back to selling vacuum cleaners."

Mr. Magruder patted her arm and said nothing. None of them wanted to leave Middleburg. They all liked it here.

There's no time to lose, Bernie thought. He had to find out more about Hazel Sutton and Thomas Valrugo.

Someone rang the bell at the front desk.

Bernie got up from the table and went to see who it was. There stood a large woman with bright yellow curls all over her head. Bernie was sure he had never seen her before, yet the voice was familiar.

"Any mail for Sutton in 205?" she asked.

Bernie checked the mail slot. "Here you are," he said, handing it to her. He watched her walk across the lobby and get in the elevator. Hazel Sutton. He was positive she had brown hair when she first checked in. He picked up the phone and dialed Georgene Riley.

"Georgene?" he said. "I've got a job for you, and this time I'll be the lookout."

13

Georgene arrived with Weasel, who had been skate-boarding in front of her house.

"This better be good," said Weasel.

"I don't remember inviting you," Bernie retorted. "The problem with you, Weasel, is that you think every lead has to uncover something. Sometimes you wait months to solve a case."

Weasel wrinkled his nose and shoved his glasses back up. "Months! Ha! I'll be an old man when they find the Mad Gasser."

"Listen." Bernie took them out back and they sat on the wall above the trash cans so they could talk in private. He told them about the note that Delores found in her purse, and then wondered if he was supposed to have kept it secret.

"You're not to tell *anybody!*" he cautioned.

"Now this is more like it!" Weasel said. "It could be the cook, or the cleaning woman, or even one of the waiters."

Bernie hadn't thought about the people who worked in the hotel. He felt dizzy with all the possibilities.

"This is what I want you to do," he said to Georgene. "Some woman was in the lobby this afternoon about the time Delores came home, but I can't remember who she was. It might have been Hazel Sutton in room 205. *This morning* she walked through the lobby with straight brown hair and this evening it was blonde and curly. I think there's a reason for her disguise. I want you to go in her room and check it out. She's up there now."

Georgene stared at him. "What do you mean, check it out? When you and Weasel checked out a room, there was nobody in it."

"Look," said Bernie, "The Besseldorf Hotel offers a 'goodnight special.' When guests sign in, we always ask if they want us to deliver something hot to drink just before bedtime, and every night we carry the drinks up. I already checked the list. Hazel Sutton has her name down for coffee every night at ten-fifteen."

Georgene looked doubtful. "So she opens the door. Then what?"

"Then you go in and put the tray on her bedside table, and she signs for it. We'll find out whether she's using blue or black ink."

"Okay," said Georgene. "That doesn't sound too hard."

"One more thing," said Bernie. "You've got to find out if she's wearing a wig."

"Oh, marvelous!" said Georgene. "How am I supposed to do that?"

"I know," said Weasel. "I saw it once in a movie. Just say, 'Excuse me, but I believe there's a spider in your hair,' and sort of tug at it. If the whole thing lifts up, you'll know it's a wig."

"Great," said Georgene, rolling her eyes.

At ten o'clock Bernie went to the hotel kitchen and asked Mrs. Verona if she needed any help with room service.

"I'll take the coffee around," he offered.

"Well, there are three ready to go now," she said, and gave him a list of names.

Bernie put the coffee on a tray and carried it into the elevator where Georgene and Weasel were waiting. They pressed the button to second, and delivered the other two coffees first. Then they headed for room 205.

"I don't know about this," Georgene said, sucking in her breath. "What if something happens?"

"I'll be right outside the door," Bernie promised. "Weasel will be watching from down the hall."

He followed her to the room and then hid behind a table in the hallway. Georgene knocked.

"Who is it?" came a voice.

"Room service," said Georgene.

The door opened and the large woman with the yellow curls stepped aside. Georgene took the tray in. Bernie crawled over to the doorway and watched.

Georgene set the tray down and handed Hazel Sutton the paper to sign. The woman picked up a pen and scribbled her name. Georgene, staring intently at something across the room, said, "Thank you," took the paper and came back out.

Bernie followed her down the hall.

"Her hair!" he said. "You forgot to check."

Georgene waited until they were inside the elevator with Weasel. "I didn't have to," she said. "Her whole dresser top is covered with wigs. She's even got one in gray. And there's a sample case beside her bed with *Wallace Wigs, Incorporated* on it. She's a saleswoman."

"Oh, for Pete's sake," said Weasel.

Bernie leaned glumly against the side of the elevator. "What color ink was she using?"

"Black," said Georgene.

Bernie sighed. The problem wasn't that there were no suspects to investigate. There were people all over the place. All he had to do was choose the right one.

14

The following afternoon, Georgene and Weasel came back to the hotel with Bernie when school was out, waiting for Thomas Valrugo to show up. Mr. Magruder said he had gone out after lunch and hadn't returned. It grew later, however, and still he didn't come.

Hildegarde went clanking through the lobby to do the back hall, waving a mop at Mixed Blessing who barked at her buckets.

"I don't think he's coming," said Georgene.

"I'll bet he's up at the parachute factory planting another gas bomb," said Weasel.

They gave up waiting finally and went back to the apartment to play Parcheesi on the kitchen table. Lester was making himself a grape milkshake. First he put a half cup of grape jelly in the blender, then a scoop of chocolate ice cream, then a small can of grape juice, and finally a package of Kool-Aid.

"For Pete's sake, Les, turn on the blender and get it over with," said Bernie irritably.

"The suspense is killing me."

Lester flipped the switch. The stuff in the blender turned gray. Bernie tried not to watch while Lester drank it.

It was just about then that it happened. Mrs. Magruder was scraping carrots by the sink, Lester was finishing his milkshake, Joseph was studying in the bedroom, when Delores came rushing in from the lobby, her face as white as a dinner plate.

"The Mad Gasser!" she said. "He's in the hotel."

Mrs. Magruder dropped the carrot, and Joseph came out of the bedroom.

"Where? How do you know?" asked Joseph.

"I can smell it! The gas! I just got a whiff."

Mrs. Magruder went to the door leading to the front desk. "Theodore," she said. "Come quickly."

Mr. Magruder put down his pen and went into the apartment.

"Call the police," Mrs. Magruder instructed, and Joseph picked up the phone. "Delores has just smelled the gas here in the hotel. Delores, now, are you sure?"

"Absolutely," said Delores. "I would know it anywhere."

Weasel's eyes opened wide with excitement. "I can smell it, too! Yuk! It's awful!"

It was indeed. Bernie clapped one hand over his nose.

"Get everybody out!" Theodore said. "I'll ring the alarm. Same plan as before. Bernie, you get the folks on first."

Everyone got safely out just as the first fire truck drove up.

Even standing outside, Bernie could smell the awful odor. Delores was right: rotten potatoes, ammonia, sick cats, sour cream, and maybe a little burning rubber.

Again the firemen raced inside wearing their gas masks, and once again the Fire Chief and Police Inspector went around with their detectors. And, just as they had before, they came back out ten minutes later, shaking their heads and looking puzzled.

John Doe went over to the Police Inspector. "Is there anything I can do to help?" he asked.

"Yes," said the Inspector. "Go back to your room and stay there." Then he picked up his bullhorn and addressed the crowd: "The Bessledorf Hotel is now free of gas," he said, pointing to the open windows and doors. "In order to help us with our investigation, we are requesting that everyone go back to wherever he was. We will interview each of you in turn. Please cooperate."

Everyone went back inside. Bernie and Weasel and Georgene took their places at the

Parcheesi game on the kitchen table. Lester leaned against the refrigerator. Mrs. Magruder went back to the sink, and Joseph sat at his desk.

"I just walked in," Delores told the police, going through it all again, "and the minute my nose hit the lobby, I smelled the gas. I walked right back to the apartment, like this, and told Mother, and she told my father. . . ."

There were footsteps outside the rear door of the apartment, footsteps going back and forth, back and forth.

"Shhhhh," said the Inspector, putting one finger to his lips. He tiptoed across the kitchen and flung open the door.

15

Hildegarde stood there with her mop and bucket.

"What are you doing?" asked the Police Inspector.

"Just what you told me to," Hildegarde snapped, plainly put out. " 'Go back to where you were,' you told me. 'What am I supposed to do?' I asked you. 'Whatever you were doing before,' you says. So I'm mopping the hall twice. You haven't had your dinner yet, you could eat off it."

"That smell!" said Delores. "It's the gas!"

The terrible odor of rotten potatoes, ammonia, sick cats, sour cream, and burning rubber began to fill the apartment kitchen.

"Close the door quickly," said Mother, dragging Hildegarde inside. "Oh, Hildegarde, is it you, then?"

The cleaning woman stared. " 'Course it's me. Who do I look like, Wilbur Wilkins?"

"Hildegarde," said Theodore sternly. "Are you the Mad Gasser?"

Hildegarde's face went as blank as melted ice cream. She stared at Mr. Magruder. "The

Mad Gasser!" she exclaimed. "Mr. Magruder, I've been called some names in my life, but nobody's ever called me that."

"Just a minute," said the Police Inspector. "Hildegarde, tell me exactly what you did a half hour before the alarm sounded. Sit down, if you like. Make yourself comfortable. Don't leave out a single detail."

Hildegarde looked warily about the room, then sat down in a chair next to the table, her hands on her mop handle.

"Well, let's see. First off I dusted the lobby and wiped the potted plants. Then I got me a Snickers bar and unwrapped it and put the paper in the trash bin and. . . ."

"Not *that* detailed," said the Police Inspector.

"Then I gets out my bucket and picks up a box of soap powder, and then I changes my mind."

"What do you mean?"

"I decided to try some of that new stuff they show on TV — *Gone* — so I opens the bottle and pours some in the bucket. Smells awful, but it's so strong, so thorough, so reliable, that even the most stubborn stains come clean."

"Oh, no!" said Mother.

"Let me see that bottle," said the Police Inspector. Hildegarde went out in the hall and returned with *Gone*.

"Stand back!" said the Police Inspector, and took off the cap. He took a whiff and reeled back against the stove. "Is this what you smelled at the parachute factory?" he asked, handing the bottle to Delores. She took a quick sniff and began to gag.

"That's it! That's it exactly!"

There was a knock on the door, and Officer Feeney stuck his head in the apartment kitchen. "We've interviewed the folks on the first floor. Want us to go up to second?"

"Hold it," said the Inspector. "Feeney, I want you to get in your car and go bring in the person who cleans the parachute factory. Call the owner and find out who it is."

Fifteen minutes later, Officer Feeney returned to the apartment with a tiny woman in a blue dress and blue apron with "Bessledorf Parachute Factory" embroidered on the pocket.

"Now what's all this?" she protested. "Ought to be ashamed of yourself — out roundin' up us folks who make an honest livin' when you ought to be out chasing down crooks and pickpockets."

"Please calm yourself," said the Police Inspector. "Tell me, have you ever seen this product?" He held up the bottle of *Gone*.

"Sure," said the woman from the parachute

factory. "It's the one on TV. 'So strong, so thorough, so realiable, that.' . . ."

"Never mind," said the Inspector. "Have you ever used it at the factory?"

"Sure have. Use it on the floor of the boiler room."

"When did you use it last?"

"Well, now, let me see. Mondays, I scrubs down the harness room, Tuesday I do the chute tables, Wednesday I sweeps up all the grommets, Thursdays. . . . Thursday, it was. I does the boiler room floor on Thursdays just before I leave for home."

"How many times have you used it?"

"Twice."

"The last two Thursdays?"

"That's right."

Officer Feeney and the Police Inspector exchanged glances.

"Well, I'll be!" said Theodore. "There's the Mad Gasser, right inside that bottle."

But Delores was not convinced. "How do you explain all the gagging and choking and fainting?" she asked.

"Well," said the Police Inspector, "just let one person think she's been gassed, and suddenly everybody's going down like a string of dominoes."

"Then the case is solved," said Bernie, hardly able to hide his disappointment.

"Not quite," said the Inspector. "There's still somebody around who calls himself the Mad Gasser."

"But we'll just tell the reporters it was all a mistake and that will be the end of it," said Theodore.

"You're not to tell anybody anything — *any* of you," the Inspector said sternly. "I would suggest that you not use the product *Gone* again, but in the meantime, we will circulate the rumor that the Mad Gasser has struck the Bessledorf Hotel, and the investigation is continuing."

"But why?" said Mrs. Magruder. "If Robert L. Fairchild finds out, Theodore will lose his job."

"If there is any problem, refer Mr. Fairchild to me," said the Inspector. "You see, we are on the trail of a man who goes about the country following unusual crimes. He poses as the culprit, demands a large some of money to stop, and then leaves town. If he finds out this was all a mistake, he'll take off before we can catch him. The last time he demanded money was after a series of fires. Turned out that someone else was setting them, but he claimed to be the arsonist and got out of town with five thousand dollars the citizens had collected to get rid of him. Now that we know he's in Middleburg, we don't want him to get away again."

Bernie looked at Georgene and Weasel. The Mad Gasser was here in this hotel, he was sure of it, and somehow they had to find him.

16

The story made the newspaper the next day.

"Bessledorf Hotel Hit by Mad Gasser," the headlines declared.

The town was in an uproar, demanding that the mayor do something.

"If they can't catch him," one man declared, "they ought to pay him what he wants and get him out of here. It'll be a school he gasses next."

When Officer Feeney stopped by the hotel that afternoon, Bernie walked with him to the park.

"What are the police going to do?" Bernie asked.

"Wait until we get another note and hope it gives us a clue," Feeney said.

"How did he get away before without anyone catching him?"

"Oh, he's a clever one, he is. Told the police to leave the money in the towel dispenser in the restroom in the back of a Greyhound bus. Well, the police did — wrapped it in a nice little bundle and stuck it in the dispenser, all right. Figured the guy was really stupid, because when that bus pulled out for Nashville, naturally, there were detectives on board, waiting to see who used the restroom."

"He'd be trapped, wouldn't he?" asked Bernie.

"Well, that's what the police thought. Every time someone used the restroom and came out, one of the detectives went in and checked. The money was always there. First thing they knew, they were pulling in the bus depot in Nashville and still didn't have a suspect."

"What happened?"

"Well, before anybody got off, they checked that money one last time and discovered that only the top layer was there, the rest had been replaced with cut-up paper towels. So they got a search warrant and checked every single person on that bus, including the driver, but nobody had the money, so they had to let them go. Found out later that the criminal, whoever it was, had taken most of the money out of the bundle and flushed it down the toilet."

"Yuk!" said Bernie.

"Oh, money washes very well. They figure he had an accomplice working in the crew that empties the tanks under the bus toilets, and that the two of them split the money fifty/fifty. Found out, too, that the men had been leaving messages for each other taped to the bottom of a table in a coffee shop. One of the notes was found, but both of the men got away." Feeney reached in his pocket for a handkerchief, and a piece of paper fluttered to the ground.

"What's that?" Feeney asked, as Bernie bent down to pick it up. And then, noting the printed letters, yelled, "Don't touch it! It's from the Mad Gasser!"

It was from the Mad Gasser, all right. Stooping over, Bernie could read the words very well:

> TELL THE MAYOR I'M GETTING IMPATIENT.
> ANSWER SOON OR I STRIKE AGAIN.
> THE MAD GASSER
> OF BESSLEDORF STREET

The printing was in the same block letters as the note before, done in blue ink. Bernie stared at it hard and noticed that the ink was smudged just a bit to the right of each letter, the way Lester's writing always looked on his school papers. But at least the Mad Gasser could spell. It couldn't be Lester.

Gingerly Officer Feeney picked the note up — the tip of one corner — and carried it carefully down to headquarters to be checked for fingerprints, while Bernie went back home.

How did the note get inside Feeney's pocket? Somehow, in the policeman's travels, the Mad Gasser had slipped it there. It had to be Thomas Valrugo, Bernie decided.

Later, just after Bernie had walked Mixed Blessing and returned him to the doormat, he saw that old Mr. Lamkin was not alone in the dining room. Sitting at a table in a far corner was Thomas Valrugo, stirring his coffee and reading a book. Maybe, this very moment, he was waiting for a chance to leave another note.

Bernie stood behind the dining room door and watched through the crack. It took Mr. Lamkin longer to eat a bowl of Jello than it took Bernie to eat a steak dinner. Every so often, Thomas Valrugo took a sip of coffee and glanced over toward the old man. And every three or four minutes, Mr. Lamkin took another bite of Jello. Somehow, Bernie decided he had to get Mr. Lamkin out of there so Thomas Valrugo would do whatever he was waiting to do, and Bernie could catch him red-handed.

He went back to the apartment.

"Lester," he said. "How would you like a huge three-decker sandwich?"

Lester looked up from the Matchbox cars

he was racing along a windowsill. "Sure, if you make it for me."

"Tell you what," said Bernie. "I'll make it for you if you eat it exactly where I tell you to."

"Okay, but it's got to have lots of mayonnaise," said Lester.

"Lots of mayonnaise. Check," said Bernie, getting out the bread.

"And some peanut butter and bacon bits."

"Right," said Bernie.

"And dill pickle and onion and salami. Hold the tomato."

When the sandwich was finished, Bernie took Lester to the door of the dining room. "See that table opposite Mr. Lamkin's? I want you to sit in that chair right there, facing him. That's all you've got to do. Just sit there and eat this sandwich. Here's a Coke to go with it."

Lester took the Coke and sandwich into the dining room and sat down at the table across from Mr. Lamkin's. He lifted the top slice of bread, sniffed it, licked off the mayonnaise, wiped his hands on his shirt, and took a big bite. Pieces of onion dangled from his lips. Bacon bits spilled down onto his plate. Mr. Lamkin stopped eating and looked up.

Lester bent over and licked up the bacon bits. He wiped his chin with the hem of his tee shirt, took another bite, and chewed with his mouth open.

Mr. Lamkin put down his spoon.

Lester took a long slurp of Coke and wiped his fingers on his pant leg. Then he took another bite, and the bottom of the sandwich fell off. He stuffed it all back in his mouth and belched loudly.

Mr. Lamkin got up, leaving his Jello behind him, and went on down the hall to his room. Five minutes later, Lester's sandwich was gone, and sucking up the last of his Coke, Lester sauntered on back to the apartment.

Bernie stood at the crack behind the door, watching. Mr. Valrugo stopped reading and looked around as someone else entered the dining room. Hazel Sutton took a table near the door and ordered coffee, too.

Thomas Valrugo went back to his book. Hazel Sutton sipped her coffee. Thomas Valrugo turned a page. Hazel Sutton checked her watch. Thomas Valrugo picked up his cup. Hazel Sutton picked up hers.

They're up to something, Bernie thought.

At some point Hazel Sutton glanced over at Thomas Valrugo and saw him studying her intently. A moment later she got up and left the room. Valrugo left soon after. There was no note left anywhere.

17

On Sunday, the third page of the paper carried an advertisement for the Bessledorf Parachute Factory, where business had dropped off sharply since the first gassing scare. The announcement said that in order to show that Bessledorf Parachutes were as safe and reliable as they had always been, there would be a dramatic, breath-taking, "act-of-faith" on Bessledorf Hill that very day at two P.M. An unnamed citizen, it said, with no previous sky-diving experience, had volunteered to leap from a plane above the factory to show the world that he trusted Bessledorf parachutes with his very life. There would also be balloons for the children.

"Dang fool thing to do," Mr. Lamkin muttered, shuffling through the lobby. "Now if you want to hear about the Flying Aces back in 1917. . . ."

But nobody did. Everyone was heading up the hill for the free show, and Bernie and his friends decided to go and take Mixed Blessing with them. It was then they discovered the dog was missing.

"Did anyone let him out?" Bernie asked his father.

"Not that I know of," Theodore answered.

"Hit the deck! Hit the deck!" squawked Salt Water.

Bernie, Georgene, and Weasel checked every floor of the hotel and the basement as well, but there wasn't a trace of Mixed Blessing. Even his leash was gone. Bernie was about to leave when the phone rang at the front desk, and he answered. It was Albert Oates.

"Tell Delores," he said, "that if she wants to see your dog again, she had better be at Bessledorf Hill at two o'clock."

Bernie told his sister.

"That blinking idiot!" Delores said. "Does he think he can change my mind doing this?"

But Lester began bawling at the idea of losing Mixed Blessing forever, so Delores put on her jacket and set out for Bessledorf Hill with Lester, Bernie, and his friends following close behind.

A large crowd had gathered. There was a huge banner above the door of the factory saying, "Bessledorf: The Chutes You Can Trust." Mr. Hokum, the factory manager, came out to say that the parachute factory was in Middleburg to stay and that no madman would force them out.

The people cheered. "And now," said Mr. Hokum, "to prove that Bessledorf Parachutes are as safe as they ever were, a courageous Middleburg citizen will put his ultimate trust in a Bessledorf chute."

As the crowd watched, a tiny speck appeared in the sky, growing larger and larger. Bernie could just make out the shape of a small plane.

It came closer and closer until it was almost over the parachute factory. At that moment a tangle of arms and legs fell out of the hatch on one side.

"It's a bird!" Bernie joked.

"It's a plane!" said Weasel.

"It's a dog!" shrieked Lester.

"It's Albert!" gasped Delores.

It was Albert and Mixed Blessing as well. Albert was on the bottom, dangling from a rope that was attached to a harness around Mixed Blessing, and the dog's harness, in turn, was attached to a gorgeous white parachute that billowed beautifully against the blue sky. Halfway down, Albert unfurled a banner, which he turned in all directions so that everyone could read it.

Delores Magruder, will you marry me? it said.

The crowd laughed.

Albert Oates reached the ground. Mixed Blessing fell on top of him, and the chute covered them both.

Delores, her face pink, rushed forward as Albert crawled out from beneath the chute. He held out his arms, but she pushed him aside, grabbing Mixed Blessing instead, and unfastened his harness.

"Albert Oates," she declared, her face turning purple, "I could have you arrested for dognapping."

"I just wanted to be sure you would come. It's the most dangerous thing I ever did in my life, and I did it all for you."

"I came, I saw, and I was disgusted," said Delores.

"This is better than the speech and the parachute jump," someone in the crowd said.

"But Delores, my dove, I belong to you alone," said Albert.

"There is only one place in the world you belong, and that is a lunatic asylum," said Delores, and marched back down the hill with Mixed Blessing trotting shakily behind her.

The crowd began to disperse. Mr. Hokum looked pleased, because so many people had turned out and the reputation of Bessledorf parachutes was once more secure.

It was that night, long after everyone else had gone to bed, that Bernie heard a message in Morse code being tapped out somewhere in the hotel.

18

The sound seemed very far away, and Bernie doubted he would have heard it at all if the hotel weren't so quiet. Twelve-fifteen. Most of the guests were in and the doors locked.

He got up softly and stole out into the living room of the apartment, listening. *Dah . . . dit . . . dah . . . dit, dah . . . dit . . . dah . . . dit . . . dit* . . . Morse code for sure. He and Weasel had studied it until they knew all the letters and numbers. Bernie opened the door leading to the registration desk.

The soft dots and dashes were coming from down at the end of the hall. Tiptoeing, Bernie went by each door, listening, until he reached Mr. Lamkin's room.

Dah . . . dit . . . dah . . . dit, dit . . . dah . . . dit . . . dah, dit . . . dah. . . .

Bernie's head spun. He tried to read the message, but the letters were coming much too fast.

The floor creaked behind him, and Bernie felt a hand on his shoulder. He whirled around. It was his father.

"What's going on?" Theodore asked.

"Listen," Bernie said, pointing toward Mr. Lamkin's door.

Theodore took a few steps forward. "Sounds like Morse code," he whispered.

"It is. I'm sure of it."

"Can you make out what it's saying?"

"No. It's coming too fast."

"Come on." Mr. Magruder pulled Bernie back down the hall to the registration desk and softly dialed the Police Inspector at his home. "Don't lose a minute," he told him. "There's something you have to hear."

Three minutes later, a car pulled quietly up in front of the hotel with its headlights off, and Theodore opened the door for the Inspector. John Doe also came in, returning from a late movie.

Theodore put one finger to his lips and led the Inspector down the hall toward Mr. Lamkin's room. John Doe followed curiously. For a moment the telegraph key stopped, then started again.

"Do you read Morse code?" Theodore asked the Inspector.

The police inspector nodded as he copied down letters on his note pad.

Bernie watched, scarcely breathing. What if this was it? What if old Mr. Lamkin were really someone else in disguise? He watched the Inspector's face anxiously.

The bushy white eyebrows began to crinkle at the corners, the lips began to stretch, and finally he handed the notepad to Bernie:

"Cloudy with a chance of rain tonight. Tomorrow, fair and unseasonably warm, high near 80. . . ."

The Inspector smiled. "I figured it might be something like this. Mr. Lamkin was a telegraph operator in the First World War, and he likes to keep in practice. Turns on the radio sometimes and transmits it in Morse code."

"Rats!" said Bernie, as they all went back to the lobby.

John Doe pressed the button for the elevator. "Still haven't caught the Mad Gasser, eh? Getting sort of embarrassing, isn't it?"

The Police Inspector's cheeks colored just a bit. "Well, we just might be closer to solving the case than anyone thinks," he said, and abruptly left the hotel.

If John Doe doesn't solve it first, Bernie thought. What bothered him was that the secret about the gas couldn't be kept forever. Sooner or later someone else would smell *Gone* and spread the word. When that happened, the Mad Gasser would catch the first bus out of town.

"If we don't find out who he is, he may give

up and leave," Bernie said to Georgene and Weasel as they sat on the school steps the next day. "We've got to trail Thomas Valrugo and Hazel Sutton this afternoon and not let them out of our sight. I think they're planning something big."

"What are we supposed to do? Sit outside their hotel rooms like watch dogs?" asked Georgene.

"I've noticed that both of them eat lunch at the hotel dining room every day, so we've got a least until one o'clock. When the bell rings at noon, I'm going to eat part of my sandwich and then tell the lunchroom supervisor that I don't feel good. After she sends me home, you go up to her and tell her you don't feel so good either. We'll meet back in the hotel lobby."

The morning dragged on. But at last the bell rang for lunch and Bernie met his friends at their table in the all-purpose room. Bernie gulped down half his sandwich.

"Now?" said Weasel.

"Now," said Bernie, and holding his stomach and looking grim, he walked slowly up to the supervisor.

"I don't feel so good," he said. "I think there was something wrong with my sandwich."

The supervisor looked down at him. "Good

heavens!" she said. "Better get down to the nurse right away."

The nurse? Bernie's stomach did a somersault, but he just nodded and went slowly out the door, then waited in the shadows for Georgene and Weasel. If they went to the nurse, she would put them on cots and keep them there for the afternoon.

He could see Georgene getting up, her face contorted as though in pain. The lunchroom supervisor stared at her and put one hand on her forehead, then nodded toward the door. Georgene went out, and Bernie whispered to her to wait for Weasel.

About five minutes later he got up, hands over his mouth as though he were about to throw up. Half the students in the all-purpose room were standing up now, watching.

"Not another one!" cried the supervisor. "What is this? An epidemic?"

She motioned him quickly out the door, and a moment later Bernie, Georgene, and Weasel were all heading down the hall toward the front entrance.

19

When they walked in the door of the hotel, Bernie wondered if he was really flushed, because Theodore looked up from the desk and said, "Bernie, are you all right? I just heard it on the radio."

"Heard what?" said Bernie, puzzled.

"About the school closing — flu epidemic, or something. Said three children left the cafeteria sick, and suddenly everyone was vomiting."

Bernie, Georgene, and Weasel stared at each other. They really had not meant to start something like that.

"Uh . . . yeah, we're fine. But we thought we'd just sort of sit here and take it easy," Bernie said, and the three sat down on the couch.

"Think I should have the doctor look you over?" his father asked.

"No, let's wait awhile and see," Bernie said, and after Mr. Magruder went back to his account books, Bernie looked at the others and said, "Whew!"

They sat for a half-hour watching the door

of the dining room. Finally a big woman in a red wig came out.

"Okay," Bernie whispered to Georgene. "Here comes Hazel Sutton. I don't know if she's in this or not, but we're going to find out. Follow her wherever she goes. Don't leave her for a minute. Sit outside her door if you have to and follow her down to dinner. We'll meet here again then and compare notes."

The heavyset woman went clomping past them, one hand holding onto her wig, pressed the button for the elevator, and got on. As soon as the door closed, Georgene scampered to the stairway to be on second when she arrived.

"Shake a leg! Shake a leg!" squawked Salt Water.

Back in the dining room, Jack Martin was starting on his second cup of coffee. Suddenly he got up and came to the door of the lobby.

"Hey," he called to Bernie and Weasel. "Would you boys go down to the drugstore and buy me a good cigar?"

Oh, no, thought Bernie. They couldn't leave now. "You go," he whispered to Weasel. "Come back as soon as you can, and I'll wait for Valrugo to finish lunch."

Weasel got up. "Sure," he said to Jack Martin, and took the money the man gave him.

Bernie took a deep breath. So far so good.

Georgene would follow Hazel Sutton, he would follow Thomas Valrugo, and. . . . And then he stopped swallowing, stopped breathing, almost, for a thought crossed his mind. He hit his forehead with the palm of his hand. He had it all wrong! Why hadn't he realized it before? There had *been* no gassing of the parachute factory, so it didn't matter who had registered just before it happened. Whoever was writing those notes and pretending to be the Mad Gasser had probably come to town *after* the story had run in the newspapers.

Weasel came back with the cigar. Jack Martin gave him a tip and went back in the dining room to finish his coffee.

"My tip," said Weasel, coming over to the couch and showing Bernie a nickel. "Boy, you sure can't get rich around here."

Bernie grabbed his arm. "Weasel, we've had it all wrong. It isn't Sutton or Valrugo we should be trailing. It's whoever checked in after word of the gassing got out."

The phone was ringing at the front desk, and Mr. Magruder answered.

"Bernie," he called over. "John Doe is checking out and wants someone to bring down his luggage. Would you and Weasel go?"

Bernie nodded, and the boys walked over to the elevator.

"Think!" said Weasel, pushing his glasses back up his nose. "Who checked in just after the story made the headlines?"

The elevator door closed, and they started up. "Someone in 302, but he's gone," Bernie said. "A woman down on first, but she's gone too. The only one . . ." He turned slowly to Weasel. "The only one who's still here is just leaving. John Doe."

"How can we stop him if we're not sure?" asked Weasel, his teeth starting to chatter.

"How would we stop him even if we were?" asked Bernie.

They moved down the hall together and knocked at the door of 315.

"Come on in," called John Doe.

Warily the boys stepped inside. The man was packing his second suitcase. The curtains billowed from the open window as the warm October air blew in.

Bernie stood by the desk and waited, his heart thumping. A blue pen lay on the desk top beside an airline ticket. As John Doe put his shoes in the suitcase and locked it, Bernie leaned forward and saw that the ticket was for a flight to New York at 2:27. And then, looking back at John Doe, he noticed something else: the edge of the man's left hand was smudged with blue, just like Lester's when he wrote on his school writing tablet.

This meant that John Doe was left-handed like Lester, and that he dragged his hand over words as he wrote them. And then with a start, Bernie remembered the note the Mad Gasser had somehow slipped in Officer Feeney's pocket and the way the printed letters were smudged.

"I guess I'm ready," John Doe said. "Each of you boys carry a suitcase, and I'll take the satchel."

There was something tense about John Doe's face — the same way he had looked the night before in the lobby when the Inspector said that perhaps they were closer to catching the Mad Gasser than anyone thought. Maybe John Doe, if he *was* the Mad Gasser, was going to make his getaway. Somehow Bernie had to slow him down, keep him from leaving until they could get the Police Inspector here.

He reached down for the suitcase and then, pretending to swing it high up onto his shoulder, let go of the handle and sent it flying right out the open window.

Weasel stared, aghast. John Doe's face grew gray as the suitcase thudded onto the roof of the funeral parlor next door.

Bernie had hoped he could make it look like an accident, but the squint of John Doe's eyes told him it was foolish even to have tried. And a moment later he heard his own voice saying,

"I know who you are, and your fingerprints on that suitcase will be safe until the police get here."

Whatever Bernie thought would happen next, however, didn't, because John Doe reached inside his coat and pulled out a gun.

"Stand right where you are, and don't make a sound," he said.

Funny little bleating noises came from Weasel's throat in spite of himself.

John Doe threw his satchel on the bed. "Open it, Bernie," he commanded, motioning with the gun.

With legs like limp asparagus, Bernie moved over to the bed and opened the satchel. There were all kinds of things crammed inside it: bullets, rope, passport, flashlight, flares, tape. . . .

Somewhere out on the street, a maintenance crew began work with a jackhammer.

"Get out the rope," John Doe instructed.

Bernie couldn't hear. "What?"

"The rope!" John Doe said impatiently.

Bernie did.

"Tie up your friend, and I mean tight." John Doe moved closer. "Put your hands behind you," he told Weasel.

"Yes, sir," Weasel breathed.

Weasel put his hands together, and Bernie tied them.

"Knot it again, and put the knot on the inside," John Doe said.

Bernie noticed that Weasel was still holding the nickel he got from Jack Martin.

"Now take off his shoes and tie his feet together."

When Weasel was tied up, John Doe moved over to the bathroom, holding his gun at Bernie all the while. He reached in and grabbed two washcloths. Then he stuffed one in Weasel's mouth. Weasel looked as though he were going to be sick.

"Tape his mouth shut," John Doe said.

Reluctantly, Bernie did.

Then it was Bernie's turn. With the gun beside him on the bed, John Doe tied Bernie's hands tightly behind him, turning the knot to the inside. He took off Bernie's shoes, tied his feet together, gagged him, and taped his mouth shut. Then he shoved both boys inside the closet. Bernie could hear the sound of the bed being pushed across the floor and slammed hard against the closet door.

The phone rang, and John Doe answered.

"Yes, Mr. Magruder, the boys were up here and took my suitcases down. No, I won't need a cab. I'm taking the bus next door. Yes. . . . Fine." He hung up.

A moment later, Bernie heard his footsteps cross the room, pause, and then go out into the hall. The door closed and the lock clicked.

20

He'll go next door and try to get his suitcase down off the roof of the funeral parlor, Bernie thought. The plane didn't leave until 2:27. At least an hour off.

That was Bernie's first thought. His second was what would happen to him and Weasel, how long it would take for them to be found. He moved his wrists. They were tied so tight that they hurt. He tried to say something to Weasel, but all that came out was "Mmmfff."

When he was sure that John Doe must be downstairs, he scooted closer to the door of the closet and banged his head against it, but that hurt. He tried banging it with his shoulder and then, leaning back, with his feet. Someone had to hear, he figured, and come.

But the rooms on either side had been vacant since Saturday. The couple two doors down had gone out shopping just as Bernie was coming up. What about the room below? he wondered. Surely someone down there would hear. And then his heart sank. The woman in that room had checked out of the hotel that morning.

He could feel Weasel climbing over him in the dark, struggling to get to his feet. Weasel rattled the door handle, trying to get it open. He grunted and pushed and banged against the door, and Bernie pushed too, but the bed had been wedged between the closet door and the dresser. The door wouldn't budge.

Stay calm, Bernie told himself, but his pulse was racing. Weasel slid down beside him, and Bernie turned so that his fingers touched the rope around Weasel's wrists. No matter how they twisted and turned, however, Bernie's fingers could not grasp the knot.

Outside the jackhammer started again and then another machine began a steady thump, bang, thump.

Bernie's fear grew. Even if they managed to get the ropes off their hands, they would not be able to open the closet door. And even if they banged with both fists and shouted, the sound could easily be mistaken for the noise outside. It might be hours before their families became alarmed enough to start a real search. He wondered when Hildegarde would do the room. Not until morning.

He leaned wearily back against the wall as the men out in the street worked on. He could figure how long he and Weasel had been in the closet by the number of buses that had passed the hotel. Two buses, fifteen minutes apart. A half hour had gone by at least. John Doe would be at the airport by now.

As Bernie's fingers touched Weasel's again, he realized that Weasel was still holding the nickel that Jack Martin had given him. And then he had an idea.

There was a water pipe that ran down through the corner of the closet to the closet below and then down to the first floor and the closet of old Mr. Lamkin's room. Where would Mr. Lamkin be now? Probably in the dining room finishing his custard. If he were through, however, the first thing he always did after lunch was take a nap. The plan might not work, but Bernie could think of nothing better.

"Mmmfff," he said again.

"Ummmphh?" Weasel questioned.

"Mmmfff," said Bernie, and wiggled his fingers across Weasel's until they reached the nickel. He gripped it hard, careful not to drop it. Then, scooting around so that his back was against the water pipe, Bernie carefully tapped out his message, using quick taps for dots, a scrape of the nickel along the water pipe for dashes and a pause between each letter and word:

Dot, dot, dot . . . dash, dash, dash . . . dot, dot, dot. . . .

S.O.S.

Slowly, laboriously, he tapped on.

Third . . . floor . . . closet.

And then: Dot, dash, dash, dash . . . dash, dash, dash . . . dot, dot, dot, dot . . . dash, dot. . . .

John . . . Doe . . . Mad . . . Gasser.

"Uhhh! Uhhh!" said Weasel, and somehow Bernie knew he was saying, "Good show!"

Bernie expected to hear shouts and footsteps as soon as the message was out. He heard nothing but the far off sounds of doors closing and the elevator clanking and, outside, the steady drill of the jackhammer.

Weasel nudged his arm. "Uhhhh!" he said.

"Ummmphhh?" questioned Bernie.

Weasel nudged him again.

Bernie slowly sent the message again. *S.O.S. . . . S.O.S. . . . Third floor . . . closet. . . .* And when it was over, he did it again and again. The minutes dragged on. He was repeating it for the fifth time when he heard the sounds that he and Weasel had been waiting for. The elevator door clanked open. Footsteps came running down the hall. Voices. Banging of the door of 315.

Bernie and Weasel pounded hard against the door of the closet with their feet. Bernie could hear his father's voice saying, "Hold on, I've got the key."

Then people were in the room, and Mr.

Lamkin was saying excitedly, "Clear as a bell! Came right down the water pipe into my closet. 'What's this?' I says to myself. 'Some kind of joke?' But it came again, and I says, 'I better go tell Mr. Magruder about this.' "

Joseph's voice: "Move that bed." And finally the door opened.

Bernie gulped with relief as the tape was removed from his mouth, and his hands and feet were untied.

"The police are on their way," Theodore said. "Take it easy, now. What can you tell us, Bernie?"

"It's John Doe, and he's got a gun," Bernie gulped.

"On the roof of the funeral parlor," said Weasel.

"Catching a plane for New York," said Bernie.

"What? What?" said Theodore. "Catching a plane from the roof of the funeral parlor?"

Bernie and Weasel ran to the window of the room, but there was no sign of either John Doe or his suitcase.

Mr. Lamkin was bobbing about like a cork in the bathtub: "Clear as a bell!" he said. "Came right through my closet. Why, it was like being back in the trenches again. 'Lamkin' I says to myself, 'you aren't over the hill yet. You still have a job to do.' "

"What time is it?" Bernie asked his father anxiously.

Theodore looked at his watch. "Two thirty-one."

Bernie slumped down on the edge of the bed.

"It's too late," he said. "John Doe caught a plane to New York a few minutes ago."

"How do you know?"

"I saw the tickets there on his desk. I couldn't think what else to do, so I threw his suitcase out the window. I wanted to stop him somehow. But it's gone, and so is he."

"We can still wire the authorities in New York, and they'll be waiting when the plane comes in," said Theodore.

They didn't bother to take the elevator, but went clattering down the stairs, Bernie blinking back tears of frustration. He had so desperately wanted to be in on the capture. Now it would all happen somewhere else.

"How did you know it was John Doe?" asked Joseph.

"Yeah," Weasel said. "What made you so sure, Bernie?"

"His hands were dirty," said Bernie. "I'll explain later."

Halfway down the stairs, they collided with the Police Inspector and officer Feeney coming up. Thomas Valrugo was with him.

Bernie stared at Thomas Valrugo, but before he could say a word, the door leading to second floor flew open, and Georgene shrieked, "I've got him! I've got him!" And in the hallway beyond, they could hear Mixed Blessing barking.

"Who?" asked Bernie, beginning to hope again.

"The Mad Gasser! It was Hazel Sutton. I peeked in her door . . . I mean his door . . . and saw her . . . I mean, him . . . shaving . . . and I ran downstairs to get the dog and tied him to the door handle and he's got Hazel . . . I mean, the Mad Gasser . . . cornered."

"It's not the Mad Gasser, it's his accomplice," said the Inspector, as Officer Feeney charged down the hall to make the arrest. "Word just came through from Detroit. Mr. Valrugo here is from the FBI. He's been following the trail of the accomplice and is sure now that he's Nicholas Bean, masquerading as a woman. All that's left to do is to find the Mad Gasser himself."

"It's John Doe, and he's on a plane to New York right now!" Bernie said. "I saw the tickets. We just didn't make it in time!"

"What?" said the Inspector, but Feeney was motioning to him from down the hall and he hurried off.

"Oh, boy! Oh, boy! This is better than the

movies!" said Mr. Lamkin.

"How could Hazel Sutton . . . I mean, Nicholas Bean . . . be the accomplice?" Bernie asked Thomas Valrugo. "She . . . I mean, he . . . was registered before the first gassing ever took place."

"We figure he was hiding out here in Middleburg from that arson extortion deal," the FBI man told him. "He didn't know I was trailing him. When a rumor started about the gassing of the parachute factory, he saw another chance to make some money and wired John Doe to come to Middleburg."

The Inspector came to the door of room 205 and called them all down. When Bernie entered, a man wearing a blue and white polka dot blouse, handcuffs, and no wig at all, was scowling at him from against the wall.

"What flight did John Doe take to New York?" the Inspector asked Bernie, picking up the bedside phone.

"The two twenty-seven," Bernie said. He walked over to the window and stared glumly down at the funeral parlor below.

There was a funeral in progress. The casket was carried out to the waiting hearse. Then the flower-bearers came with the wreaths and floral sprays, and finally the mourners themselves in somber shades of blue and brown. The tall men in the dark suits patted them on the shoulders and ushered them to the long black cars.

Bernie was about to turn away when he saw a large floral wreath near the door of the funeral parlor start to move. He stared down at it. It went a few paces and stopped and then a few paces more, dipping and rising and dipping again.

"Weasel," he whispered. "Come here."

Weasel and Georgene came over to the window while the Inspector was talking to New York.

"Look at those flowers," said Bernie.

"They've got feet!" said Georgene.

The flowers were moving toward one of the cars in the funeral procession and suddenly a stocky man, limping badly, wearing a blue overcoat, darted out from behind the flowers and got into the waiting car.

"It's him!" yelled Bernie. "The Mad Gasser!"

The Inspector dropped the phone.

"He didn't get away after all. He must have hurt his leg getting down off the roof of the funeral parlor and hid inside," said Weasel.

The Inspector and Thomas Valrugo rushed to the window.

"Where? Where?" they cried.

"In the funeral procession," said Bernie. "Stop him!"

They turned just in time to see Nicholas Bean trying to creep out the room in his polka dot blouse and handcuffs, but they caught him, tied him up, and tore down the stairs and out the door just as a police car with two more policemen arrived.

"What's this?" asked the head mortician, as the Inspector flagged down the hearse just as it was about to leave the driveway.

But Thomas Valrugo was creeping up behind the fourth car in the procession, and a moment later, John Doe, alias the Mad Gasser, threw his gun out the window in surrender, while the mourners on either side of him there in the back seat fainted dead away.

A cheer went up from the door of the Bessledorf Hotel where the Magruders, the cook, the handyman, and the waiters were all watching. And while Thomas Valrugo and the two policemen took their two suspects into custody, the Inspector came back to the lobby to get a statement from Bernie about how it all had happened.

"The funny thing is," the Inspector told them, "John Doe's real name is John Doe. So one thing we *can't* prosecute him for is using an assumed name. And Nicholas Bean had the perfect disguise. Nobody's going to suspect a woman who wears a different wig every day and doesn't try to hide it. Not unless somebody catches her shaving her chin, that is."

"Why did John Doe decide to leave town?" Weasel asked.

"I guess he felt things were getting a little too hot. The notes would go on, though, through Nicholas Bean; but if things got too risky for him, he would leave, too. Well, they'll both be going now, back to Detroit to face charges." He reached out his hand and shook Bernie's. "Let me congratulate you, Bernie. You're the youngest detective we ever had on a case!"

"Don't forget Georgene and Weasel," said Bernie. "They were in on it, too."

The Inspector shook hands all around. Even Mixed Blessing was not forgotten. He was given all the chipped beef left over from lunch for his help in capturing the accomplice.

At that moment, however, Bernie noticed a note under the doormat, and picked it up.

"Dear Delores," it read. "I have gone to Hoboken to devote my life to my uncle's suspenders. If you ever change your mind, there will be a place for you here as my wife. Albert." Bernie took the note to Delores. She picked up a pen and wrote at the bottom:

Dear Albert:

Thank you for your kind sentiments. I

am happy to know that you are holding up well in your uncle's suspenders factory. I will marry you when the Mississippi River wears rubber pants to keep its bottom dry.

As ever,
Delores

Then she put it in an envelope and stamped it.

All afternoon people came and went; newspaper reporters and photographers; even Mr. Fairchild flew down from Indianapolis to congratulate the hotel staff. Mr. Lamkin went from one to another:

"Clear as a bell, I heard it," he said to anyone who would listen. "There I was, just taking off my shoes, and I says, 'Hey, what's this? Sounds like some kind of code coming from my closet.' Just like being back in the trenches again. Why, in 1917. . . ."

Bernie shook hands with the reporters, signed a few autographs, posed for pictures beside Georgene and Weasel, and finally, because he was feeling so good, sat down by Mr. Lamkin and asked what he had done in the war.

The employees of Thorndike Press hope you have enjoyed this Large Print book. All our Large Print titles are designed for easy reading, and all our books are made to last. Other Thorndike Press Large Print books are available at your library, through selected bookstores, or directly from the publishers.

For more information about titles, please call:

(800) 223-1244
or
(800) 223-6121

To share your comments, please write:

Publisher
Thorndike Press
P.O. Box 159
Thorndike, Maine 04986